Waltham Forest Libraries

Please return this item by the last date stamped. The loan may be renewed unless required by another customer.

June 18		
	WITHDRAWN	

With special thanks to Anne Marie Ryan
For Reg Wright and Richard Maskell, who
granted my wish of becoming a writer.

ORCHARD BOOKS

First published in Great Britain in 2018 by The Watts Publishing Group

1 3 5 7 9 10 8 6 4 2

Text copyright © Hothouse Fiction, 2018
Illustrations copyright © Orchard Books, 2018

The moral rights of the author and illustrator have been asserted.

A CIP catalogue record for this book
is available from the British Library.

ISBN 978 1 40835 111 6

Printed and bound in Great Britain by Clays Ltd, St Ives plc

The paper and board used in this book are made from wood from responsible sources.

Tropical Party

ROSIE BANKS

Wishing Star Palace

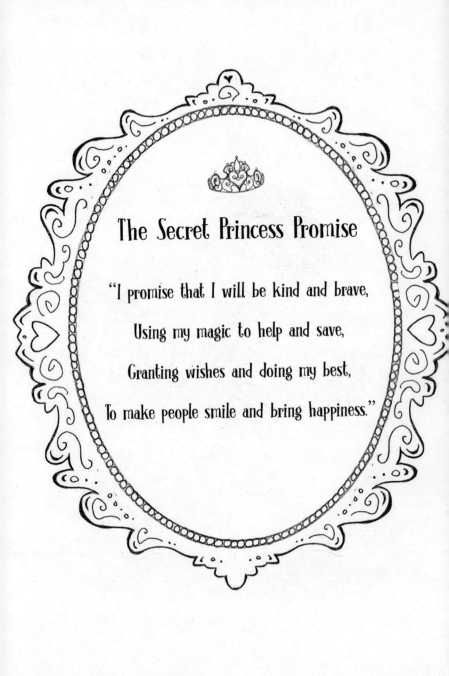

The Secret Princess Promise

"I promise that I will be kind and brave,

Using my magic to help and save,

Granting wishes and doing my best,

To make people smile and bring happiness."

CONTENTS

CHAPTER ONE

Grandma's Gift

"You look gorgeous, Mum!" said Mia Thompson.

Mia's mum was sitting at her dressing table putting on glossy red lipstick, while Mia and her little sister, Elsie, perched on her bed watching her get ready for an evening out with friends.

"You smell good too," said Elsie, sniffing

the air as Mum dabbed perfume behind her ears. "Like flowers."

Smiling, Mum turned around and squirted a bit of perfume on the girls. Then she twisted her hair, which was blonde like Mia's, into an elegant bun. As she looked at her reflection in the mirror, Mum frowned. "Hmm. Something's missing," she said.

"How about this?" suggested Mia, going over to the dresser and getting a beaded necklace.

As Elsie clomped around the bedroom in Mum's high heels, Mia fastened the necklace around her mum's neck. It sparkled against her new black dress.

"Perfect!" said Mia.

"It's not as pretty as yours," Mum tapped the gold half-heart necklace that Mia always wore and winked.

DING DONG! The doorbell rang.

"Gran's here!" shouted Elsie, kicking off Mum's shoes and charging downstairs to answer the door.

Mia followed Elsie downstairs and gave

her grandmother a big hug, breathing in Gran's comforting scent. "Hi, Gran," she said happily.

Mum clattered downstairs in her high heels. "Be good for Gran," she told the girls.

"We will," promised Mia.

"Don't stay up too late," said Mum, grabbing her clutch bag.

"We won't," said Elsie.

Mum kissed them both goodbye, leaving lipstick marks on their cheeks.

"Have fun," called Gran, as Mum hurried out, shutting the door behind her.

"Now come and play, Gran!" said Elsie, tugging her grandmother's hand.

"I think I need a cup of tea first, Elsie,"

said Gran, laughing.

As she waited for the kettle to boil, Gran set her bag down on the kitchen counter and started singing. "Oooh! I'm gonna be a star," she crooned, pretending a spoon was a microphone.

"What are you doing, Gran?" asked Elsie, giggling.

"I'm being a pop star, like your old babysitter," joked Gran.

It was true. Alice, who used to babysit them, was now a famous singer. She'd won

a TV talent show and performed concerts around the world.

Elsie danced around the kitchen, singing Alice's latest hit at the top of her lungs.

"How about you, Mia?" asked Gran, sipping her tea. "Do you still like Alice's music?"

Mia nodded. "Charlotte and I are Alice's biggest fans."

Charlotte Williams was Mia's best friend who lived in America. She and Mia didn't just love Alice because of her singing. They loved her because she'd given them the most amazing opportunity ever – a chance to become a Secret Princess like her!

Secret Princesses used magic to grant

16

people's wishes. Shortly before Charlotte had moved to California, Alice had given the girls special necklaces and invited them to Wishing Star Palace to begin their training. Hidden away in the clouds, Wishing Star Palace was a magical place where the Secret Princesses met. Even though the girls now lived far apart, they got to meet at the palace – and it was all because of Alice!

Of course Mia couldn't tell Gran any of this, because Secret Princesses kept their magic a secret. But she did say, "We're really lucky to be friends with Alice."

Finishing her tea, Gran said, "Oh! I nearly forgot – I made you presents."

"Yay! Presents!" squealed Elsie, clapping her hands.

Gran rummaged in her bag and handed them each a soft parcel. The girls eagerly tore off the wrapping paper and found hand-knitted blankets inside. Mia's was turquoise and Elsie's was lilac. But they weren't ordinary blankets, they were shaped like—

"Mermaid tails!" cried Elsie. She sat down and pulled the blanket over her legs. She flapped the blanket as if it was a tail.

"Thanks, Gran," said Mia, stroking the woolly blanket. Its stitches were designed to look like scales. "These are so cool."

Elsie wriggled on the floor, pretending she

was swimming. "I've always wanted to be a mermaid."

Mia smiled at her little sister. Unlike Elsie, she already knew what it was like to be a mermaid! Not long ago, Mia and Charlotte had met four mermaids at Wishing Star Palace. The Secret Princesses had used

their magic to give the girls temporary tails so they could swim with the mermaids in the beautiful Blue Lagoon. It had been incredible to swish through the water like fish – they'd even been able to breathe and talk underwater!

Mia swallowed hard, remembering what else that had happened on that visit. As she and Charlotte had swum in the Blue Lagoon, a poisonous frog had jumped in and turned the water green and smelly. The frog had been sent by Princess Poison, the Secret Princesses' enemy. She'd once been a Secret Princesses herself, but she had been expelled for using her magic to become more powerful instead of helping people.

The only way to break her horrible curse on the mermaids' home was to grant four watery wishes.

Mia glanced down at her necklace and shivered with excitement. Three aquamarine gems shone out of the half-heart pendant – rewards for the three watery wishes she and Charlotte had already granted. But it looked as if they'd have a chance to earn another one soon, because the pendant was glowing!

"Um, Gran, can you teach me how to knit a mermaid tail blanket?" Mia asked.

"Of course," said Gran.

"I'll just go and get my knitting things," said Mia, dashing out of the kitchen. She hurried into her bedroom and shut the door. She knew that Gran and Elsie wouldn't even notice she was gone, because time would stand still while she was with the Secret Princesses.

Clutching her pendant tightly, Mia said, "I wish I could see Charlotte."

The glow from her pendant grew brighter, filling her bedroom with dazzling light. It swirled around Mia, carrying her towards her best friend … and adventure!

Grandma's Gift

When she arrived at the palace, Mia was
wearing a beautiful golden dress, sparkling
ruby slippers and a diamond tiara. Seconds
later, a girl in a pretty pink dress appeared
in the grand entrance hall. A tiara just like
Mia's rested on top of her brown curls.

"Hi, Charlotte!"
called Mia, her ruby
slippers clicking on
the marble floor
as she ran to greet
her friend.

Throwing her
arms around
Charlotte, Mia
heard a faint noise

coming from the magic moonstone bracelet on her wrist.

"Hello?" she said, speaking into the milky white stone.

"It's Princess Phoebe," said a voice coming from the stone. "Please come to the swimming pool right away – we've got a mermaid emergency!"

CHAPTER TWO
Mermaid Medicine

"I wonder what's wrong?" said Mia, her blue eyes wide with worry.

"We'd better go and find out," said Charlotte, grabbing Mia's hand.

The girls clicked the heels of their ruby slippers together three times. "The swimming pool!" they cried.

The magic whisked them to a spectacular

swimming pool surrounded by palm trees. The pool had twisty slides and a trickling waterfall, but the most amazing thing was the mermaids swimming in its clear, turquoise water! Since Princess Poison's frog had poisoned the Blue Lagoon, the palace's mermaids had been forced to leave their home and move to the swimming pool. But not all of the mermaids were in the water …

A young mermaid with light-green hair was lying by the side of the pool. Her face looked pale and the silver scales on her tail had lost their usual sparkle. She smiled weakly when she noticed them.

"Oh no!" cried Mia, hurrying over. "What's wrong with Marina?"

A Secret Princess with curly hair and
a white coat over her dress was crouched
down next to Marina, a stethoscope around
her neck.

"Marina's not feeling very well," said
Princess Phoebe, who was a doctor back in
the real world.

"She's been really tired lately," said Coral,
a mermaid with coppery red hair and a
shimmering purple tail.

"And she's lost her appetite," said Oceane,
a mermaid with silvery hair and a glittering
green tail.

"She didn't even want to try my special
sea-salt caramel cookies," said Princess
Sylvie sadly.

"Wow, she must feel bad," said Mia. Princess Sylvie, who had a pendant shaped like a cupcake on her necklace, made the most delicious magical treats.

"We hoped a visit from you two might make her feel better," said Nerida, a dark-haired mermaid with a turquoise tail.

"We're here now, Marina," said Charlotte soothingly, taking the mermaid's hand. Mia stroked Marina's hair gently while Princess Phoebe examined her.

"Stick out your tongue and say 'ah'," said Phoebe, peering inside Marina's mouth.

Phoebe looked into Marina's ears. Then she took the mermaid's temperature and listened to her chest with the stethoscope.

"Hmm," said Princess Phoebe, putting her stethoscope away in her doctor's bag.

"Is Marina sick?" asked Mia, her eyes filling with tears at the thought of her friend being unwell.

"She's not sick," said Phoebe. "She's just homesick."

Marina nodded sadly.

"Luckily, I have just the right medicine for her," said Phoebe.

"You do?" asked Marina, looking surprised.

"Oh yes," said Phoebe. She whispered something in Princess Ella's ear.

Ella waved her wand and suddenly three small furry creatures appeared on the side

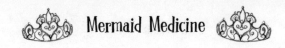

of the pool. Their black noses twitched as their beady eyes regarded the mermaids and princesses curiously.

"Otters!" cried Mia, recognising the adorable animals.

The otters slid into the pool, squeaking happily as their sleek bodies streaked through the water. Without hesitating,

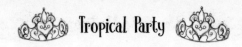

Marina dived into the water after them.

"Fetch!" cried Marina. She threw a ball across the pool. The otters took off like a shot, racing to retrieve it.

"Otters love to play," said Princess Ella, who was a vet back in the real world.

So did Marina!

"Good boy," said Marina, beaming as one of the otters brought the ball back to her. Her cheeks looked pink and, as she swished her silver tail through the water, it sparkled in the sunlight.

"Marina's looking better already," said Charlotte.

The young mermaid giggled happily as one otter nuzzled her face with its whiskers

and another
splashed her with
its little paws.

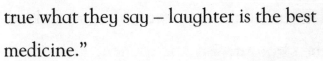

"I thought you
said you needed to
give Marina some
medicine" said Mia.

"I did," said
Princess Phoebe,
smiling. "It's
true what they say – laughter is the best
medicine."

Mia and Charlotte took their ruby slippers
off and dipped their feet in the cool water.
They watched the otters whizzing down the
pool slide on their bellies and splashing the

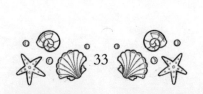

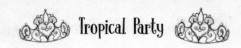

mermaids as they landed in the water.

"I wish we could play with the otters too," said Mia longingly.

"We just need to grant one more wish to earn our aquamarine combs," said Charlotte. "Then we'll be able to turn into mermaids whenever we want."

"And we'll have broken Princess Poison's curse," said Mia.

"What are we waiting for?" Charlotte said, scrambling to her feet. "The sooner we grant a watery wish, the sooner Marina will be back home!"

Putting their slippers back on, the girls clicked their heels together three times and called out, "The Magic Pearl!"

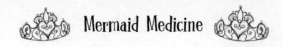
The magic took them to a coral cave
lit by the soft pink glow coming from an
enormous pearl. Mia glanced beyond the
cave's entrance at the slimy green water.
"The Blue Lagoon still looks terrible," she
said. Pinching her nose, she added, "And it
smells bad too."

"Not for much longer," said Charlotte,

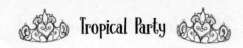

pulling her towards the pearl.

The image of a girl with a red flower tucked into her thick black hair shimmered on the pearl's surface.

As Mia and Charlotte touched the pearl, a message appeared:

Kala's made a wish
by the water so blue.
Say her name to help make it come true!

"Kala!" the girls cried in unison.

Magical bubbles rose up around the girls,

lifting them away from the cave – and towards the girl whose wish they needed to grant.

A moment later, the girls found themselves in a tropical garden. The air was hot and humid, with a hint of a sea breeze. A sign said *Molokai Community Garden*.

"We blend in perfectly," murmured Mia. The flowery dresses they were both wearing matched the exotic blooms all around them.

A mountain rose up in the distance, but much closer by was the girl from the pearl! Kala had her back to them and was standing on her tiptoes, trying to reach something hanging from a tree branch.

"Let me help," called Charlotte, running

over. She stretched up and plucked a ripe mango off the branch, then handed it to Kala.

"Thanks so much," Kala said, adding the mango to a basket. She gave the girls a big, friendly smile that reached all the way to her dark eyes. "And aloha!"

CHAPTER THREE
Fruity Fun

"Aloha?" Mia said uncertainly.

"What does that mean?" asked Charlotte.

Kala laughed merrily. "You can't be from Hawaii if you don't know what aloha means."

"We're just visiting," said Charlotte.

"Aloha means hello," explained Kala.

"But it's also an attitude. The aloha spirit means being kind and caring. It's about getting along with everyone."

That sounds a bit like being a Secret Princess, thought Mia. Secret Princesses did magic, but the most important part of their job was being nice and helping others.

"I'm Charlotte, by the way," said Charlotte.

"And I'm Mia," said Mia with a shy smile.

"Nice to meet you," said the girl. "My name is Kala."

"What are you going to do with all that fruit?" asked Mia, peering into the basket. It was full of tropical fruit – bananas, mangoes, melons and others that Mia had

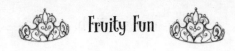
never even seen before.

"It's for a luau," said Kala. When she saw the blank expressions on their faces, she laughed again. "That's the Hawaiian word for party. My family is throwing a surprise

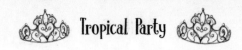

luau for my grandparents tonight – it's their ruby wedding anniversary. They've been married for forty years."

"I bet they'll be pleased," said Mia.

"I hope so," said Kala. "I really wish it will be the best surprise party ever."

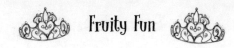

Charlotte caught Mia's eye and winked. They'd only been here a minute but they'd already discovered what Kala had wished for! Now they just had to make the wish come true.

"Can we help?" offered Mia.

"Are you sure?" asked Kala. "I don't want to keep you from exploring the island."

"We're positive!" said Charlotte. "Besides, it'll be fun to explore Hawaii with you!"

"That's true," said Kala. "Well, if you really don't mind, you can help me pick more fruit."

"Do you need some of these?" asked Mia, pointing to a tree with clusters of oval-shaped fruit growing at the top.

"Oh, yes," said Kala. "Papayas are my grandmother's favourite."

Charlotte reached up to pick a green fruit, but Kala called out, "Not that one – only the yellow ones are ripe!"

The girls picked all the yellow papayas they could find, while Kala picked glossy green fruits with ridges.

"Those look like stars," commented Mia.

"That's why they're called starfruit," Kala said, giggling.

She led Mia and Charlotte over to a row of plants. Each one had a pineapple sprouting out of the middle of its leaves, like a prickly flower. Kala sniffed one of the pineapples.

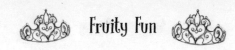
"What are you doing?" asked Charlotte.

"Checking whether it's ripe," said Kala.

Mia and Charlotte sniffed the pineapples closest to them.

"This one smells good," called Mia.

"Let's hope it tastes as sweet as it smells!" Kala said, cutting the pineapple off its stalk.

When they'd picked a few more pineapples, Kala looked down at her basket. "I think I've got enough fruit," she said. "Now I just need to cut it all up for the party."

"We can help with that, too," Charlotte said quickly.

"Really?" said Kala. "That would be great. I live just over there." She pointed to a pink

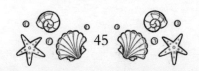

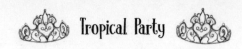

house across the street from the garden.

As they helped Kala carry the fruit home, Mia asked, "Does the whole garden belong to you?"

"Oh no," said Kala. "It's a community garden. We share it with our neighbours. My brother, Keanu, and I help look after the plants."

"Cool," said Charlotte.

"I'm home!" called Kala as they went inside the house. The girls followed her into the kitchen, where they set the basket of fruit on the counter. From the kitchen window, there was a stunning view of sparkling blue water. Kala's house was right on the beach!

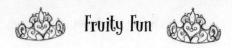

A dark-haired woman was taking a cake
out of the oven.

"Mum, these are my new friends Mia and
Charlotte," said Kala. "They're going to
help me prepare the fruit."

"Aloha," said Kala's mum, smiling at the
girls. "It's very kind of you to help us out.

It means I can finish making Kala's outfit for the party tonight."

Kala's mother left the kitchen and the girls got busy chopping up fruit.

"Hey, what do you get if you cross an apple with a Christmas tree?" asked Charlotte as she trimmed the prickly skin off a pineapple.

"I don't know," said Kala, looking puzzled.

"A pineapple," said Charlotte.

"Ha!" laughed Kala. "Good one. I'll tell it to my grandfather tonight."

Mia sliced open a papaya. There were lots of black seeds inside. "Is it supposed to look like this?" she asked.

"Yep! Scoop out the seeds," Kala told her.

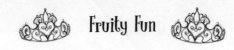
"And cut off the skin."

"I've never had papaya before," said Mia as she sliced the fruit.

"Seriously?" said Kala. "You've got to try it!"

Mia bit into a piece of papaya. "Mmm," she said, as a sweet flavour filled her mouth.

"What should I do with this?" asked Charlotte, holding up a hot pink fruit with leathery green leaves.

"That's a dragon fruit," said Kala. She grinned. "But don't worry – it won't hurt you."

She cut the dragon fruit in half, revealing firm white flesh speckled with tiny black seeds.

"It reminds me of kiwi and pear mixed together," said Charlotte, crunching a piece.

"It's not warm enough where I live to grow all these yummy fruits," said Mia.

"It's not just the weather," said Kala. "Things grow well here because of the soil. It comes from volcanoes."

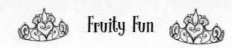

"Volcanoes?" said Charlotte.

Kala nodded as she sliced a mango. "The mountain you can see in the distance is a volcano. It's supposed to be where Pele lives."

"Who's Pele?" asked Mia.

"She's the Hawaiian goddess of fire," explained Kala. "According to the legend, she had a big fight with her sister, the sea goddess. She got angry and her volcano erupted. The lava that flowed out formed Hawaii when it cooled."

"Wow," said Mia. "Sometimes I get annoyed with my little sister, but I can't imagine getting that angry at her!"

Kala grinned. "Yeah, you definitely don't

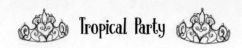
want to get on Pele's bad side. There's a superstition here about Pele's Curse – if you offend the goddess of fire, you'll supposedly have bad luck."

"We'll be on our best behaviour," joked Charlotte, cutting up the last pineapple. When all the fruit was chopped up, the girls arranged it on platters, making colourful patterns.

"This looks so pretty," said Kala. "Malaho. That means thank you."

A croaking noise came from the other side of the kitchen. The girls turned and saw a fat green frog in the doorway. Its throat puffed out and its eyes bulged threateningly. It was Princess Poison's frog, Toxin.

RIBBIT!

Even though she didn't speak frog, Mia
knew it meant only one
thing – trouble!

"How did you
get in here?" said
Kala. She stepped
towards the frog
to shoo it away, but
Charlotte grabbed her
arm and pulled her back.

"Don't touch it, Kala!" she warned her.

"Why?" asked Kala, confused. "It's just a
frog, isn't it?"

Toxin jumped across the kitchen and
sprang up on the counter. Then the frog

hopped on the platters, squashing the fruit under its webbed feet. Anything Toxin touched instantly started to rot. To the girls' horror, all the fruit turned mouldy and green. Soon the beautiful fruit looked completely disgusting.

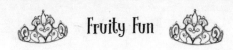

"That's why," said Mia grimly. "It's a poisonous frog."

Fruit flies started to swarm around the decaying fruit. Toxin's long tongue shot out as he hopped around the kitchen, trying to catch the flies.

"We need to get Toxin out of here!" cried Charlotte.

Mia flung open the back door. Charlotte ran around waving her hands, sending a cloud of fruit flies outside. When Toxin bounded after them, Mia quickly slammed the door shut. "Phew," she said. "Don't worry, he's gone."

"But the fruit is all ruined," said Kala. "Now we won't have any for the party."

"Oh yes, you will," said Mia. She turned to Charlotte, holding her necklace. It was time to make a wish!

CHAPTER FOUR
Lovely Leis

The girls joined their pendants together, the two halves forming a glowing golden heart. "I wish for lots of yummy fruit for the party," said Mia.

Magic shot out of the heart and the rotten fruit vanished. A flower cart appeared in the kitchen, laden with colourful bouquets.

"Huh?" said Mia, feeling totally confused.

"That's not what we wished for." She ran over to the cart to take a closer look. To her surprise, the flowers were made out of fruit! Pieces of pineapple and papaya, melon and mango had been cut into flower shapes and threaded on to skewers. The beautiful bouquets were edible!

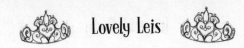

"Oh my gosh!" said Kala, staring at the fruity flower display in astonishment. "What just happened?"

"We made a wish," said Charlotte. "To fix the fruit."

"But how?" said Kala. "Are you goddesses or something? You know, like Pele?"

"No," said Mia. "We're not goddesses, we're Secret Princesses."

Kala's mouth gaped in surprise. She curtseyed to the girls. "Your royal highnesses," she said.

Mia and Charlotte giggled.

"What?" asked Kala, looking puzzled. "Isn't that what you're supposed to do when you meet a princess?"

"Well, actually, we're not princesses yet," said Mia. "We're still in training."

"And anyway, we're not that kind of princess," said Charlotte. "Secret Princesses use magic to help grant people's wishes."

"This is like something out of a story," said Kala, her eyes shining with excitement. "My brother is going to be so impressed when I tell him you guys can do magic."

"You can't!" said Charlotte quickly. "We're Secret Princesses – nobody but you can know about our magic."

Kala pointed at the cart and frowned. "How am I supposed to explain that?"

"Nobody will question it," Mia assured her. "That's just how the magic works."

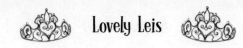

"We came here to grant your wish of throwing your grandparents the best ever surprise party," said Charlotte.

"OK!" said Kala excitedly.

"So what else can we do to help you?" asked Mia.

Kala thought for a moment. "Well, I still need to make some leis."

Now it was Mia and Charlotte's turn to look confused.

"Flower necklaces," explained Kala. "In Hawaii, we wear leis at parties and special occasions."

"They sound gorgeous! We'd love to help you make them," said Mia. She loved doing all kinds of craft projects.

"Can't you just do that magic thing with your necklace again?" asked Kala. "That would be a lot faster than making them all by hand."

"We could," said Charlotte. "But we don't want to waste our magic. We only have enough to make three small wishes – and we've already used one."

Kala packed some things in a beach bag.

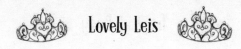

Then she gave Mia and Charlotte each a
basket and they all went out to the back
garden. It was like a tropical paradise,
with brightly coloured flowers growing
everywhere.

Charlotte swung her basket as they
headed down a path lined with wooden
statues. "She looks grumpy," said Charlotte,
pointing at a statue with a scowling face.

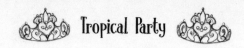

"That's Pele," said Kala. "My dad carved those statues – he's good at woodwork."

At the end of the path Mia gasped when she caught sight of the beach. Tall palm trees swayed gently in the sea breeze, while aquamarine waves lapped at the shore.

"It looks like a beach from a magazine – except the sand is black!" exclaimed Mia. She'd only ever seen yellow sand before.

"That's because it comes from volcanic rock," said Kala.

"Yo, Pele!" joked Charlotte, waving to the mountain in the distance.

Mia sniffed the air and shot a nervous look at the volcano. "Um, can anyone else smell smoke?"

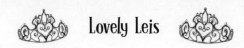

"Don't worry. It's not coming from the volcano," Kala said, laughing. "It's coming from the firepit." She led the girls on to the beach, where a man and a boy were standing by a big hole in the sand. They both wore shorts and tropical-print shirts.

"Hi, Dad. Hi, Keanu," said Kala. "Mia and Charlotte have been helping me get ready for the luau."

"Aloha!" said Keanu. His smile was just as friendly as his sister's.

Mia peered down into the hole and saw that it was filled with rocks glowing red with heat. A smoky, meaty scent wafted up from the fire, making her mouth water.

"Is it OK if they stay for the party, Dad?" Kala asked.

"Of course," her dad said, chuckling. "How else will they get to get to sample my famous barbecued pork?"

"The meat is wrapped in banana leaves and slow-cooked in the firepit," said Keanu.

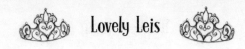
"It's totally worth the wait."

Mia's tummy rumbled in anticipation.

As Keanu and his dad went off to set up a
tent, the girls picked bright pink and purple
hibiscus flowers from bushes by the beach.
When their baskets were full of flowers,
Kala spread a picnic blanket on the sand
for them to sit on. She showed the girls how

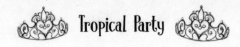

to sew the flowers into a necklace, using a needle and thread.

"Sew through the bottom of the flower," instructed Kala. "That way the petals won't fall off."

As they sat in the sunshine making leis, Kala told them more Hawaiian stories. Time flew, and soon they had each made a pile of flower garlands.

"They can't do magic like your necklaces, but they look pretty," Kala said, putting a lei around her neck.

"And smell good

68

too," said Mia, inhaling the flowers'
fragrance.

Kala's mother came down to the beach.
She held up a grass skirt. "I finished it!"

"My costume!" squealed Kala, holding the
skirt up to her waist. "I'm doing a special
hula dance for my grandparents tonight,"
she informed the girls. "This is what I'm
going to wear."

"It's beautiful," said Mia.

"Do you need a hand with the leis?" asked
Kala's mum.

"No, we've got it under control," said
Kala.

"Then I'll see if Dad and Keanu need any
help with the tent," said her mum.

The girls' baskets were empty, so they picked some more flowers. When their baskets were full of hibiscus blossoms, they headed back to the blanket to make some more leis.

"Where is everything?" Charlotte asked when they got back. The blanket was bare – the leis and Kala's grass skirt had disappeared.

"Maybe they blew away?" said Kala, sounding puzzled.

As the girls searched the sand for the missing things, Kala pointed to a short, tubby man standing next to the firepit. "He's really early for the party," she said.

The man turned around and Mia groaned.

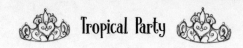

He wasn't a party guest – he was Princess Poison's nasty assistant, Hex.

And he was throwing their beautiful flower leis on to the fire!

CHAPTER FIVE
Hula Girls

Hex laughed as he threw flower necklaces into the flames. Then he held up the grass skirt Kala's mother had made.

"Stop!" shouted Kala, waving her arms wildly. "That's my costume!"

Ignoring her, Hex tossed the hula skirt into the fire.

"No!" cried Kala, sinking to her knees.

Mia and Charlotte sprinted to the firepit, but it was too late to do anything – the grass skirt and all the leis had already turned to ashes.

"That was a nasty thing to do," Charlotte told Hex angrily.

Hex shrugged. "I was just trying to help. The fire needed some more fuel."

"You weren't trying to help," said Mia. "You don't even know what that means."

"Can't take the heat?" Hex hissed at the girls. "Then you should go. Because Princess Poison is going to do everything in her power to stop you two from granting another wish."

Kala stared at the burnt remains of the

flower necklaces, shaking her head in disbelief. "Don't you know it's bad luck to burn a lei?" she said.

"That's just a silly superstition," scoffed Hex.

But as he strode off across the black sand, a coconut fell off a palm tree.

CLONK!

It hit Hex on the head.

"Ow!" he cried.

"That's got to hurt," said Mia, wincing as Hex rubbed his head. A big red bump was forming on his head.

"Serves him right," said Charlotte.

"I did try to warn him," said Kala.

"Trust me," said Charlotte, "Hex deserves all the bad luck he gets. He – and that poison frog – work for someone called Princess Poison. They're trying to spoil your wish."

"But we're not going to let them," Mia added quickly. She glanced at the water, thinking of the Blue Lagoon. It wasn't just for Kala's sake that they needed to grant her wish – it was for the mermaids, too. Marina needed to go home!

"What are we going to do?" said Kala. "There's not enough time to make the leis again. And my mother will be so upset when I tell her what happened to my skirt."

"We didn't want to use our magic to make leis," said Charlotte, "but now I don't think we have any other choice."

Mia and Charlotte held their magical half-heart pendants together. "I wish for the things Hex burnt to be replaced," said Charlotte.

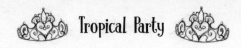

Light blazed out of the golden heart.
Suddenly the picnic blanket was covered
in leis. Not even one square of tartan was
visible under the piles of flower necklaces.

"Oh, thank you!" cried Kala, whose
clothes had transformed into a grass skirt
with a red strapless top. There was a lei
around her neck, a crown of red and yellow
flowers on her glossy black hair, and
matching flowers around her wrists and
ankles.

"You look gorgeous," said Mia.

"So do you!" said Kala.

Mia looked down and gasped. She and
Charlotte were wearing hula outfits, too!
They each had grass skirts, a beautiful lei

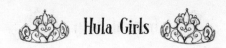

and a flower tucked behind their ear.

"Oh, wow!" said Charlotte, swishing her grass skirt.

"Now that you look the part, you should learn how to hula," said Kala. She dug a mobile phone out of her beach bag and pressed a button. A gentle, lilting tune

started to softly play.

Kala swayed to the music, taking little steps and turning her waist in circles. "You try too," she urged the girls.

Mia and Charlotte copied Kala's moves as she tapped her feet and shimmied her hips.

"Good," said Kala. "Now for the arms." She raised her arms and made wavy movements with her hands.

"Every movement has a meaning," explained Kala. "So a hula tells a story."

She raised her hands above her head. "This means the sun." Then she stuck her left arm out and bent her right arm at the elbow, gracefully circling it around her head. "And this means the wind."

Waving her hands in front of her like a flame, she said, "Can you guess what this means?"

"Fire!" said Charlotte.

"Good!" said Kala. She held up her hands, palms facing out, and moved them up and down, gently wiggling her fingers. "How about this one?"

"Rain!" exclaimed Mia.

Kala beamed. "That's right!"

Mia and Charlotte practised the hand

movements Kala had taught them.
Charlotte did dancing at home, but Mia
was normally a bit shyer. But she loved hula
dancing!

"The movements can express feelings,
too," said Kala. She crossed her arms over
her chest as she swayed. "This means love."

"This is so much fun," said Mia, crossing
her arms over her chest. "It's sort of
relaxing."

"It was supposedly invented by Pele's
sister," said Kala. "The sea goddess did a
hula dance to calm Pele down."

Charlotte glanced over at the volcano
and grinned. "I guess it didn't work."

"Do you mind if I practise the dance I'm

going to do for my grandparents?" Kala
asked them.

"Of course not," said Mia.

The girls sat on the sand and watched
Kala dance to the sound of strumming
ukuleles. Her movements were so smooth
and flowing they made Mia think of water.
Her thoughts turned to the mermaids again.

"I wonder how Marina's doing," she whispered to Charlotte.

"I'm sure she's fine," Charlotte reassured her. "The Secret Princesses are taking good care of the mermaids."

The girls clapped when Kala finished. "Your grandparents are going to be so surprised," said Charlotte.

"I really hope so," said Kala.

So did Mia. They really needed to earn their last aquamarine!

Just then, Kala's brother and father came walking down the sand, carrying a small boat above their heads.

"Come and see what my dad made for their anniversary present," said Kala.

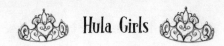

Keanu and his father set the boat down on the sand. It was a wooden canoe, polished until it gleamed. The words *Leilani and Kai* were carved inside a heart on the side of the boat.

"Those are my grandparents' names," said Kala.

"It's beautiful," said Mia.

"Thanks," said Kala's dad. He tousled Keanu's hair. "We got them a big screen TV too, but it's important to remember our culture."

"We carved the boat from a single tree trunk," said Keanu.

The sun was just beginning to set, painting an orange glow across the horizon.

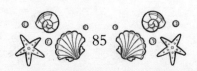

"Right," said Dad. "We should probably go in and get changed for the party."

"I'm already dressed," said Kala. "So can I take Mia and Charlotte out for a quick paddle?"

"I don't see why not," said her dad. "Just stay close to the shore."

Mia and Charlotte helped Kala push the canoe into the warm water. They all waded in and climbed into the boat. Taking turns paddling, they floated around the little bay.

"Hey, look," said Kala. "Someone's watching us."

A tall, thin woman in a green dress was standing on the beach, staring at them. Even from a distance, Mia could feel the

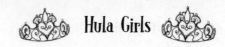

hate in the woman's cold, green eyes.

"That's Princess Poison," she said quietly. "The one we told you about."

Kala shuddered. "Thank goodness she can't get us out here."

Still glaring at them, Princess Poison waded into the water.

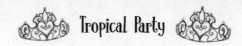

"What's she doing?" Mia said nervously.

Princess Poison twisted her black hair into a bun and secured it with a comb. There was a shimmer of green light and, as the girls watched in dismay, her legs turned into a dark green tail!

"Oh no!" cried Charlotte. "Princess Poison has turned into a mermaid!"

CHAPTER SIX
A Nasty Surprise

Princess Poison dived into the water and started swimming towards the canoe with powerful strokes.

"Hurry!" shouted Kala, paddling frantically. "Let's get away from her!"

But Princess Poison's tail propelled her through the water much faster than the girls could paddle.

Princess Poison's head popped out of the water beside the canoe. Up close, Mia could see the white streak in her black hair.

"You look surprised to see me, girls," Princess Poison said, swishing her glittering green tail through the water. "Didn't you realise that I had a magic comb, too?"

She tilted her head, showing off her comb, which was studded with spiky green jewels.

"Oh yes," gloated Princess Poison. "Anything the Secret Princesses can do, I can do better."

"No, you can't," said Mia. "The Secret Princesses help people – you just hurt them."

"You don't deserve that comb," said Charlotte, holding a paddle like a weapon.

Princess Poison flicked her tail angrily. "I'll tell you who doesn't deserve a magic comb," she hissed. "You two! You'll never get them either, because I'm going to spoil Kala's wish."

She grabbed the pendant shaped like a poison bottle that hung from her necklace and spat out a spell:

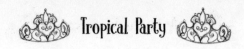

My magic is stronger than you think
Pierce this canoe and make it sink.

Green light shot out of the necklace and
bored into the side of the canoe, making
a hole right where Kala's grandparents'
names were carved. Water flooded into the
canoe.

Princess Poison laughed bitterly. "You
wanted a surprise – now you've got one!"
She dived into the water and disappeared.

The girls tried to plug up the hole but it
was too big – water kept gushing in. Soon it
had reached their ankles. Kala desperately
baled water out with her hands, but Mia
and Charlotte had a better plan.

The girls held their pendants together.
The glow coming from the heart was very
faint, as there was only a little magic left.

"I wish for the canoe to be repaired," said
Mia.

The last of the magic shone out of the
golden heart. The hole disappeared and
not a drop of water remained in the bottom
of the canoe, which looked even more

impressive than before. The seats now had scarlet silk cushions and a stunning display of red flowers spilled over the front of the boat. Tied to the back of the boat was a bunch of red, heart-shaped balloons with the message *Happy 40th Anniversary* on them.

"You saved my grandparents' gift!" said Kala.

"Maybe we should head back now," suggested Charlotte.

Kala nodded, steering the canoe towards her house. "Guests will be arriving soon."

Mia and Charlotte exchanged anxious looks. Mia knew that Charlotte was also wondering whether any uninvited guests

would turn up at the party. If Princess Poison made another appearance, they no longer had any wishes left to stop her.

Reaching the beach, the girls got out and dragged the canoe up the sand. Then, gathering up all the leis, they headed back to the house. The fruity flower cart had been wheeled outdoors and parked next to a big white tent with a buffet table. The smoky scent of barbecued meat mingled with the sweet perfume from the garden's flowers.

Kala's mother came out of the house wearing a loose tropical-print dress. She was carrying a huge hollowed-out watermelon filled with fruit punch.

"Just in time," she said, setting the watermelon down on the buffet table.

"How was your boat ride?" Kala's dad asked as he carved the meat from the firepit.

"We got a bit wet," replied Kala, winking at the girls.

DING DONG!

The first guests had arrived! Kala's parents answered the door, then led a small group of people out to the garden.

"Aloha!" Kala said, putting a lei around each guest's neck. Mia and Charlotte handed out glasses of fruit punch decorated with little paper umbrellas. As night fell, more and more friends and relations arrived.

"Listen up, everyone!" called Kala's mum.

"The guests of honour will be arriving any minute. They think they're coming here for a quiet dinner. When we bring them outside, shout 'surprise'."

DING DONG!

"Shh!" said Kala, putting her finger to her lips. "They're coming!"

Everyone waited in silence as Kala's parents went to answer the door. Mia felt a sharp elbow jab her in the side. Squinting in the dark to see who it was, Mia saw green eyes glittering in the moonlight. "Watch me spoil the surprise," Princess Poison bragged. "I don't even need magic to do it."

Princess Poison filled her lungs, ready to shout out and ruin the surprise, but

Mia acted fast. She clamped her hand over Princess Poison's mouth. "And I don't even need magic to stop you this time," she whispered.

"Mmmph!" came Princess Poison's muffled reply.

When a white-haired couple walked out of the back door, Kala's dad flicked a switch and strings of beautiful fairy lights lit up all around the garden.

"Surprise!" everyone shouted.

"Good heavens!" said Kala's grandmother, putting her hands to her mouth.

"Oh my," chuckled Kala's grandfather, wiping his eyes. "We weren't expecting that!"

Kala and Keanu went over to their grandparents, presenting them each with a lei. "Happy anniversary!" they said.

Kala's father lit bamboo torches along the garden path, their flickering flames dancing in the dark.

"Before we eat, we have a few more surprises in store," said Kala's mum, leading the guests down the path.

As everyone walked down to the moonlit beach, Princess Poison sneered, "I've got a

surprise of my own lined up, too."

Mia's tummy churned with worry. What was Princess Poison planning?

On the beach, Keanu proudly presented his grandparents with the canoe. "Dad and I made this for you."

"It must have taken you ages," said his grandmother, running her fingers over the carved names.

"I can't wait to take it out fishing," said his grandfather.

"You were right about the magic," Kala whispered to the girls. "Not even Keanu notices anything different about the canoe."

After everyone had admired the boat it was time for Kala's hula performance.

"Congratulations, Grammy and Gramps," said Kala. "I made up this dance especially for you."

As Keanu and their parents strummed ukuleles, Kala began to sway her hips to the music. As everyone watched, her graceful hands began to tell the story of her grandparents' love.

"She's doing a great job," said Mia. She glanced over at Kala's grandparents, who were holding hands and grinning happily.

Kala waved her hands in front of her body.

Charlotte frowned. "I don't remember this bit of the dance."

Kala did the movement again – and again. She stared at Mia and Charlotte, an urgent look in her eyes.

"What does that movement mean?" asked Mia, trying to remember. In a flash it came to her – *FIRE!*

She spun around and saw Princess Poison and Hex holding flaming torches at the end of the path.

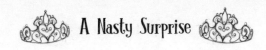
"Oh no," she muttered, as Princess Poison and her assistant started towards the house.

The girls raced after them.

"Stop!" Mia shouted.

"Put those torches down right now," ordered Charlotte.

RIBBIT!

Toxin jumped in front of the girls, blocking their way. Hex sniggered mockingly.

"Face it," Princess Poison taunted. "You're outnumbered!"

"Be careful!" said Mia. "You're going to start a fire."

"Exactly!" said Hex. "That's the plan. Then the party will be ruined."

Mia gasped. Princess Poison's surprise was even more terrible than she had imagined!

Charlotte caught her eye and shook her head. Mia gave a nod in reply. This was one of the worst things that Princess Poison had ever tried to do. There was no way that

they would they let her start a fire!

The girls moved at exactly the same time.
Charlotte tried to wrestle Hex's torch away
from him, while Mia lunged for Princess
Poison's.

"Hasn't anybody ever told you kiddies not
to play with fire?" growled Princess Poison,

swinging her torch. Mia ducked just in time. The flame missed her, but licked at the wooden statue of Pele's head.

WHOOSH!

The statue of the Hawaiian volcano goddess was on fire!

CHAPTER SEVEN

Home Sweet Home

Within seconds, the wooden statue of Pele was engulfed in orange flames. The wood crackled and popped as the blaze spread down the statue's body.

"Now this party's on fire!" said Princess Poison, a nasty gleam in her eye.

"We've got to put it out!" said Mia. They couldn't let the fire spread to Kala's house!

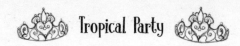

Charlotte ran towards the tent.

"What's the matter?" Hex jeered. "Can't take the heat?"

Mia wasn't sure what Charlotte was doing, but she knew one thing – her best friend was no coward. Sure enough, Charlotte came sprinting back holding the watermelon.

SPLASH! She flung fruit punch on the burning statue.

HISS! The fire went out.

"Oh, so you're trainee firefighters now, too," said Princess Poison sarcastically. "You might have saved that ugly statue but you're not going to save this party."

"Ugly?" said Mia. "Do you really not

know who this is?"

Princess Poison and Hex looked at her blankly.

"It's Pele," said Mia. "The Hawaiian fire goddess. And she has a very bad temper." She winked at Charlotte, hoping she'd play along. "Haven't you ever heard of Pele's Curse?"

"That's right," said Charlotte. She pointed to the mountain in the distance. "Pele lives in that volcano and if you insult her, she gets angry."

"What nonsense," said Princess Poison.

"Really, really angry," said Mia.

"Actually," said Hex, sticking his flaming torch in the ground, "they might be right."

He rubbed the big red bump on his head.

"Can we have some volcano sound effects, please?" Mia whispered into her magic moonstone bracelet.

There was a loud rumbling noise.

Toxin and Hex trembled in fear. Princess Poison lowered her torch uncertainly.

"Oh dear," said Charlotte. "Pele doesn't sound very happy. If I were you, I'd leave Hawaii as fast as you can."

RIBBIT! croaked Toxin. He jumped into Princess Poison's arms, covering her with poisonous green goo.

"Ugh!" said Princess Poison.

"Looks like you're already starting to have bad luck," said Mia, stifling a giggle.

RUMBLE!

Another loud noise came from the direction of the volcano.

"Let's get out of here!" wailed Hex.

Princess Poison waved her wand and the baddies vanished in a flash of green light.

"Phew!" said Mia.

"That was brilliant," said Charlotte. "We totally tricked them."

"With a bit of help from the Secret Princesses," said Mia, smiling. "Thank you!" she called into her bracelet.

The girls hurried back to the beach and caught the very end of Kala's hula dance. As her hips rocked, making her grass skirt flutter, she crossed her arms over her chest, telling her grandparents that she loved them.

"Yay!" cheered Mia and Charlotte. The rest of the audience applauded loudly.

Kala's grandparents hugged her.

"That was wonderful," said her grandmother delightedly.

"This has been the best surprise ever," said her grandfather.

As Kala beamed with pride, fireworks shaped like flowers burst out of the volcano's crater. Bright pink orchids, purple hibiscus blossoms and orange lilies lit up the night sky with sparkles.

"Ooooh!" gasped the guests, assuming that the fireworks were all part of the entertainment.

Mia and Charlotte grinned at each other. They knew the magical fireworks meant Kala's wish had been granted.

Then Mia suddenly noticed something else sparkling in the dark – her ruby slippers! Charlotte's ruby slippers had

appeared on her feet, too.

"I think the princesses want us to come back to the palace," Mia murmured to Charlotte.

The girls went over to Kala to say goodbye.

"You were amazing," Mia told Kala. "Thank you for warning us."

"No, you two were amazing," said Kala. "You stopped that bad lady and granted my wish. Now let's go and enjoy the party – you've got to try my dad's barbecue pork."

"I wish we could," said Charlotte sadly. "But we need to go now."

"It's been really fun getting to know you," said Mia.

"You two might not be Hawaiian," said Kala. "But I've never met anyone with more aloha spirit!"

Kala hugged the girls goodbye, then ran back to join the rest of the guests in the tent. Alone on the beach, Mia and Charlotte clicked the heels of their ruby slippers together three times and called out, "Wishing Star Palace!"

The girls' magic shoes delivered them

straight to the Blue Lagoon. To their delight, it really was blue again! Every trace of Toxin's slimy green poison had vanished. The water sparkled clear and blue in the sunlight. Best of all, the mermaids were back swimming in it!

"They're here!" cried Marina when she spotted the girls.

"Three cheers for Mia and Charlotte," cried Oceane.

"Hip hip hooray!" the mermaids and Secret Princesses all cheered.

"Congratulations, girls," Princess Alice said, giving them both a kiss. "You've earned your final aquamarines." She touched her wand to Mia's pendant, and then to Charlotte's. A brilliant blue jewel appeared in each necklace, next to the three aquamarines already there.

Mia reached for Charlotte's hand and gave it a happy squeeze. This was the moment they had been waiting for!

"Hurry up!" cried Marina, slapping the water impatiently with her tail. "Give them their aquamarine combs."

Alice raised her eyebrow. "Someone's eager to play with you." She waved her wand and light swirled around the girls. The four aquamarines vanished from their necklaces, but now the girls each held a jewelled comb in their hands.

"It's gorgeous," Mia said, holding her comb up to the sunlight.

"Can we try them?" asked Charlotte, her brown eyes dancing in anticipation.

"Of course," said Alice. "We'll all join in."

Grinning at each other, Mia and Charlotte tucked the combs into their hair.

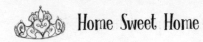

Mia felt her legs tingle, and with a shimmer of light, they became a pearly pink tail!

"Awesome!" exclaimed Charlotte. Her legs were now a glittery gold tail!

The girls slipped into the lagoon excitedly. Wriggling their beautiful tails, they swam out to the mermaids.

"It's so good to be home," said Oceane.

"Thank you so much," said Coral.

"We'll never forget what you did for us," said Nerida.

"We won't let you forget," Charlotte teased. "Now that we have our aquamarine combs we'll visit you all the time!"

"Goodie!" cried Marina.

"This is incredible!" Charlotte said, turning a somersault.

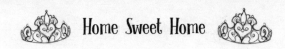

"I know!" Mia replied, blowing bubbles.

When the girls resurfaced, they saw that the Secret Princesses had become mermaids, too. Alice had a red tail, matching the red streaks in her strawberry-blonde hair.

"So what's the next stage of our training, Alice?" Mia asked her. She didn't think she could feel any happier.

"Actually," said Alice, "you two have proved that you're more than ready to become Secret Princesses. There are just two special wishes for you to grant before your princess induction ceremony."

Mia and Charlotte stared at Alice in surprise and then ...

SQUEEEEE!

Holding hands, the girls swam around in circles, squealing with excitement.

"We're going to be Secret Princesses!" shouted Charlotte.

Alice grinned at them. "Well, not this very minute. You're going home now."

"Aww!" said Charlotte. "But it's so fun swimming with the mermaids."

"We'll get to do it again soon," Mia reminded her. "Now that we have our aquamarine combs."

The girls squealed again. The mermaids and Secret Princesses covered their ears.

"I'm sending you home before you burst our eardrums," joked Alice.

"Bye, everyone!" the girls called as Alice

waved her wand, sending the girls back to
the real world.

A moment later, Mia was back in her
bedroom. Grabbing her knitting bag, she
hurried back downstairs. Elsie was cuddled
up next to Gran.

"I love being a mermaid," Elsie said,
wriggling her legs under her mermaid
blanket.

"So do I," said Mia happily. Pulling her
own mermaid blanket over her legs, she
snuggled up to Gran and Elsie, a huge smile
on her face. Soon, she wouldn't just get to
be a mermaid – she'd be a princess too!

The End

Charlotte and Mia just need to grant
two more wishes to get their
Secret Princess wands!

Find out what happens in *Princess Prom*,
two magical adventures in one!

Hula Dancing

Want to learn how to hula? It's easy! Just put on a lei, grab a grass skirt and start swaying to the music.

1. Play some hula music. (You can find songs on the internet.)

2. Holding both arms out to the right, take two steps to the right.

3. Holding both arms out to the left, take two steps to the left.

4. Gracefully raise your arms over your head.

5. Now put your hands on your hips.

6. Raise your right arm in the air and slowly turn to the right.

7. Now raise your left arm in the air and slowly turn in the other direction.

8. Repeat!

In hula dancing, each movement has a meaning.
Try out these moves, inspired by nature.

Wind
Hold one arm out to the side.
Bend your other arm at the
elbow and slowly circle it
around your head.

Rain
Hold your hands out in front
of you, palms facing out.
Now gently wriggle your
fingers as you move your
hands up and down.

Sun
With your palms facing in,
raise your arms over your
head to form a ball.

Palm Tree
Bend your right arm and lift
it in the air. Bend your left
arm and rest your right elbow
on it. Move your right hand
gently, like a tree swaying in
the breeze.

Secret PRINCESSES

What would you wish for?

Are you a Secret Princess?
Join the Secret Princesses Club at:

secretprincessesbooks.co.uk

Explore the magic of the
Secret Princesses and discover:

♡ Special competitions! ♡
♡ Exclusive content! ♡
♡ All the latest princess news! ♡